AF278800

Unpolished

by

Ramona Polivka

AuthorHouse™
1663 Liberty Drive, Suite 200
Bloomington, IN 47403
www.authorhouse.com
Phone: 1-800-839-8640

First published by AuthorHouse 4/29/2008

ISBN: 978-1-4343-8302-0 (sc)

Printed in the United States of America
Bloomington, Indiana

This book is printed on acid-free paper.

The broad shouldered Paul Bunyon type barreling down the side of the gathering hall like a runaway freight train skidded to a stop at the table where I was seated. Looking to the eldest woman he asked, "Who is the redhead Clara?" After introductions, he went on his way talking to everyone at the different tables. And, I felt as if my heart had dropped to my toes.

Who was this man that he could cause this kind of reaction in me?

Another request for dinner next week and since I had so enjoyed the discussion, I said yes. From there the relationship was in forward drive. From dinner. we progressed to long rides through the valley while he told me of his dreams for the future. He showed once a week at my house for dinner and if we stayed in he more than once told me that I made him extremely nervous when I looked him in the eye. What is wrong with looking directly at you? It just makes me very nervous. Well I am sorry but since I have impaired hearing I have learned to look directly at people when I am involved in conversation. Looking at a person's facial expressions is a big help in following conversation. He readily accepted that.

Our excursions involved such episodes as driving through Silver Falls State park in the evening hours to count the deer herds that gathered in the parking lots in fall and winter to be fed. These herds, beautiful creatures that they were, never seemed to spook at that little yellow Bug that was parked nearby. We encountered these herds on more than one occasion.

There was also the night time drive of 100 miles to go net fishing for smelt. Since I had never done that I was a willing pupil. Once was enough. To this day I intensely dislike the smell of that fish. A day spent climbing the hills of the Tillamook Burn area in the coast range and finishing up with a picnic lunch was a spectacular look at the power of Mother Nature. These interesting jaunts were never marred by alcohol and I never saw any indication of a hangover so I began to wonder if my lady friend had been wrong.

He began to call me on a regular basis several times week and wanted me to spend my free time which wasn't much with him. Our conversations ran the gamut from naughty children, and farm life to philosophy and politics. Romantic episodes were never on the agenda and while I accepted the gentle good night kisses I often wondered why he did not try to go any farther than that behavior.

We had been keeping company for about six months when one night as he brought me home, he said, "We have to have a serious discussion." He pulled into the darkened driveway and I settled back for what I expected was going to be this 36 year old man telling me that he had an ex-wife and children tucked away somewhere in his background. After all, he was 36.

Instead I got one walloping surprise. The conversation went like this, 'You know we have been going together now for six months and we have many similarities. We are Benedictine educated, country reared, same religion. I think you should considered marrying me because I think we could have a good life. Don't say yes but think about it until I come back next week.'

Well next week was only a phone call and some strange vibes coming off my mother who wondered aloud what was wrong with me. I told her I had some serious thinking to do and wasn't sure what I was going to do about an upcoming contract for the next year. Her comment was that I shouldn't do anything stupid. Well gee thanks mom I really needed that input.

I knew this man was not particularly passionate and that even that seemed to run in cycles Were passion and emotions separate entities? Could I have one without the other? Since everything he had been saying was so clinically inclined I really did wonder if he was lacking in emotions. He seemed to equate everything he did down to a moral level and was always talking about emotional control soI did have some serious doubts but when he showed up at the end of 2 weeks I said yes to his rather clinical proposal.

He talked and I listened as he told me how we should proceed. First he would ask Dad's permission to marry me…I said that I was legal and didn't need that permission. He said it was the polite thing to do, which he did the following evening during dinner. Dad got a goofy look on his face and said that I could do what I wanted.

My job expired in June so we decided that the last weekend would be a good day to marry. Since my mother had a very minimal kind of wedding she pulled out all the stops and we invited over 200 people most of whom I did not know. I would have been satisfied with something simple but she insisted on a sit down dinner followed by a dance. That part was so important to her that I let it be.

When it came time to recite vows before the pastor in church he began to stutter rather badly. Under my breath, I murmured along with the priest and that seemed to soothe Wence's stumbling. Once we were in the vestibule of the church, one of the wedding party chirped, "Aren't you going to kiss her?" Wence snapped "Not in front of all of you."

The reception that followed was somewhat traumatic for him and he held on to my hand the entire time as if I were his lifeline and got worried when my brothers got in his face and started all the kinds of teasing that men do to one another. He blushed furiously and if he had not they would not have kept after him. He did not feel comfortable around the guys for a long time afterward.

The wedding night on the Oregon coast was ….well…read on… We were settled into our suite and we sat and talked and shared a bottle of champagne. He was eager to get on to the bedroom and when his release came, he said, "Now we are really married. Do you think you are pregnant? Not likely since he never even found the target . He quickly dropped off to sleep and I lay there wondering why this was supposed to be such a fun thing to do together. Every night the same question and every time I had to say not likely. It took until the fifth night before he ever connected with his target area. I kept wondering if what I had observed as an intense respect for women was actually an innocence because he knew zilch about women It took many years before he would share his naked body in the light or look at mine.

The first time back to work the guys all ragged on him and with all the ribald jokes and innuendo he lost his cool. One of the men made some sexual remark about this new woman in his bed and he grabbed the man by the neck and literally lifted him off the floor. The man moved on shortly thereafter. That night when Wence came home to tell me what had happened. I was shocked. What kind of man had I married?

Adjusting to life in the city was difficult, but adjusting to my new husband became a daily almost discouraging task .All of the normal stresses of everyday life seemed to overwhelm him on a regular basis. Add to that the idea of a woman in his life every day, a need to find a home worthy of purchase, and the intense need to impregnate the wife and it is easy to see why he could not relax without at least 3 bottles of beer each evening. When we had spent 3 months looking to purchase he finally found what HE was looking for...a foreclosure and ready for occupancy. Well so he thought On closer investigation it was obvious that we had a job ahead of us. I refused to live there until it was cleaned up. Life in the basement was a challenge for me but since he had always lived in a room in the basement dugout when he was growing up this 6 months sojourn in the basement did not bother him.

I had experienced a miscarriage and was again pregnant and he became so overly anxious that the only way he could control the anxiety was to up the amount of beer that he consumed each night. And so began the cycle of booze and bedwetting. The more anxious he was the more beer (as much as 12 bottles in a 3 hour period) he consumed and the more often the bed was wet. I was still largely pregnant when a family member taught him how to make wine and that became his self medication. Some smart aleck said to me that I should learn to drink with him. With a baby on the way? I didn't think so.

The odd hours of labor and the C-section delivery took almost as much of a toll on him as it did on me. He was more than pleased when we were able to come home within a week and had already made arrangements for the child to be baptized. We came home on a Friday and that affair happened on Sunday. Good thing I had healed in a hurry, as I was able to attend the affair without difficulty.

Daddy was intrigued by his daughter, and as he watched what would be considered normal development by others, struck this besotted daddy as a sign of superior intelligence. I could not convince him otherwise. He would take her out of the crib in the evenings after his nap, and read aloud to her from the newspaper. He was bound and determined to start another pregnancy as soon as the dr. said it would be ok. I would have preferred a little space between babies but he said that changing two diapers would not be anymore problem than changing one. So Laura was all of four months when I found out we were having another baby. His comment, "Well, I'll be dammned." Since he had been putting out so much extra effort into this endeavor that remark annoyed me and I asked if he thought that he wouldn't be able.

That was an incredibly difficult pregnancy…morning sickness every day all day for the entire nine months…and an inability to keep more than 3 or 4 teaspoons of food down. He became worried and more than a little solicitous. Trying to tempt me with good foods that he picked up on the way home from work finally went by the wayside when he dropped a five pound jar of peanut butter in the driveway and splattered that and glass all over the place. I was relieved that the effort stopped. However, the stress of a second pregnancy was taking its toll. He now came to bed every night with the intention of sexual pleasure for himself on his mind. From start to finish was never more than three minutes and I began to hate his approach. The fact that he had consumed anywhere from six to ten bottles of beer meant that he had difficulty maintaining his function and it was always my fault when he collapsed. Trying, over and over, to push a wet noodle through the eye of a needle was no way to score points with a spouse. I found that if he thought I had climaxed, it was over more quickly. I became adept at moans, gasps, whimpering and his ego inflated more. He thought he was fantastic and I was thankful when he was asleep and I could go sit in the living room and wonder how I could teach this different soul that intimacy was supposed to be reciprocal. From the beginning and throughout this entire marriage it has never been and at some point, I quit trying. It just wasn't worth the emotional trauma.

The weather that particular summer had heated up to the three digit numbers and it was the end of August and time to schedule the C section to welcome number two. Josef was nearly 23 inches long and weighed nine pounds and several ounces. I knew something was not the way it should be well before we were released from the hospital. The nurses laid if off to new mother syndrome. Baloney! As it turned out Josef was a very cranky baby, never sleeping more than two hours at a time. The problem was a formula that didn't set well and when that was changed he did sleep better but was still a cranky baby. It took several years of hit and miss thinking until we finally discovered that Joe was allergic not only to many foods but to most everything in the outdoors. When I followed the doctor's advice and invested in vitamin supplements I thought I was going to lose my head or at least my hearing as W managed to scream at me for an entire night. Those times when he was so obnoxious I would go to the basement laundry room and cry out my frustration there. I would not give him the satisfaction of knowing he had upset me. By the time I went back upstairs evidence of tears was gone and he was none the wiser, ever because he was not as aware as he claimed to be.

By the time Josef was born so many of Wence's odd little habits had me wondering what drummer he marched to because he never did the expected So many things he did were cause for amusement in my family Perhaps it was a blessing in disguise that he never knew how amused they were.

Since we had decided that we were going to have three children, Wence made sure that his forays into physical intimacy were as often as possible. Because he did not have a clue that intimacy should be a shared venture, I put up with his physically hurtful pursuits and more often than not spent the next day or two with a decided limp. I was really glad when we got pregnant again. The stress of having survived two miscarriages and three pregnancies had turned the man into an unthinking jerk. That is not a nice way to put it, but he was.

❧

Despite his lack of social knowledge and his often inappropriate responses, he was and still is my best friend. Not only did we discuss world affairs, our church problems, our opinions of the rest of the human race,: these discussions always ended with him expecting me to agree with his opinions one hundred per cent. I told him that I was entitled to my own thoughts and he did not agree. His conclusion; Since you are my wife you will think like I do. NOT A CHANCE!

He cared but did not know how to act on that caring. At ten months Laura came down with her first ear infection and after a half hour of non stop crying I insisted on a trip to the doctor. He took us against his better judgment. The poor baby had a major ear infection. Even though we had insurance through his employment, on the way home he snarled about what this would probably cost. The child spent the next eight years with chronic infections and a bear of a parent who thought I was an ass for seeing that she got to a doctor.

From his first pediatric visit until nearly a year had passed, I had to take Joe in for a weekly head measurement. When the doctor was satisfied that the child was growing proportionately we were able to stop that task.

About the time that the children were a daily handful, the oil embargo struck and this man went bonkers. The idea of waiting in line for gasoline (even though it was only a Volkswagen that he drove) was making him act bizarrely. He came back from a wait and totally lost his cool when I informed him that the doctor had ordered me into the hospital. What am I supposed to do? I have to go to work. I found a sitter across town and it took an hour to get the kids to her house. The first time ever that Laura was with a stranger proved to be a big trauma. He then dropped me off at the hospital and made sure that he got to work on TIME. The doctor came to my room after the procedure to tell me that there was way too much tissue for this miscarriage to have been only one fetus. When I asked if he was saying twins he responded, "Or more." And was very emphatic about more spacing between the next attempt to Wence that meant sleeping in the spare bed until such time as we were ready for another baby. That was very satisfactory to me.

I was still washing diapers in a wringer machine and lugging them up the stairs to hang outdoors because we did not have a dryer. When Joe was nine months we started another pregnancy because Wence declared that at our age we needed to finish a family as quickly as possible.

Once again we had a bigger than average baby. Marie was once ounce under nine pounds. After the sickly baby that was Joe, it was a pleasure to deal with a pleasant baby. After two miscarriages and three babies within a 3 year period the doctor was adamant that this was enough. Several visits with our clergyman and the moral ethicist at the hospital and Wence agreed that the doctor was right and we stopped at three babies.

Three babies were a full time job but so was being a wife to a man who viewed everything in his life with the same intensity. Nothing was ever normal. If someone rated an event as 6 Wence was sure to label it a 10. Whether it was pouring a cup of coffee, chopping wood for the fireplace or getting ready for work, every event in his life had a consistent rating of 10 and I suspect that sometimes it was more. Is it any wonder that he could never relax enough to enjoy life?

Trying to handle all this pressure, without losing my cool, had my stomach in a constant state of upset. After a visit to the doctor it was determined that I should probably have my gall bladder removed. When Marie was four months old I spent a week in the hospital doing just that. Wence was beside himself and only came to the hospital once and that was to ask how to deal with my sister. She and her four small children had moved in to care for my family during this time. I came home and after three days I sent sister home. If I moved carefully, I could get down on the floor to diaper the children while Marie spent that period of time in her crib all day. With my sister gone, Wence was a willing helper After ten days it was time to go back to the doctor to have the stitches removed. And, then, my helper reverted to his old habits.

The doctor had put restrictions on my activities but by Christmas time I was feeling totally recovered. Good thing that the doctor didn't know what was really going on. I used to wonder what he thought of a man who would not come to be with his spouse during surgery and who thought a well person should never grace the entrance of a hospital. In retrospect I now know that the doctor was an amateur psychologist whose thoughts were similar to Wence. Women were available for the sole purpose of serving men. Hah!

Relating to his children was such a stress to Wence that the self medicating delusions of alcohol increased as the children started to pass the baby stage. The beer guzzling went down as he switched to wine. That did nothing to decrease neither the hangovers nor the bedwetting In fact, bedwetting was such a regular event that I kept a blanket in the living room because I was often jolted awake as he relieved himself all over the bed. He was trying to maintain but since he didn't know how to do that, he became short tempered and was expecting mature behavior from the kids before they were even walking well.

Then there was the need for a new roof on the house and he determined that any roofer would cheat him so he decided to do it himself. Not only did it take him an entire summer to do this, but, he dragged tar from the roof through the entire house every time he came in. I was beside myself because this was a brand new expensive carpet. Any kind of negativity on my part would have done absolutely no good. When the chore was finally finished I hired a cleaning service to shampoo the carpet while he was at work. I was not about to live with that tacky mess or have crawling babies in that goo. And honest Abe's truth…he never noticed that the rug was now clean.

What was I learning about this man? His parents were deceased when I came upon the scene and no matter how much I probed he absolutely refused to tell me anything about them. I was more than a little insulted because I felt what he could tell me about the parents would have been a big help in understanding him. I began to wonder about his awareness of the world.

As soon as Marie was born I started pushing the idea that male and female children did not share a bedroom. By the time she was 18 months old,we had found a larger adequate home ;not what I particularly wanted but one which he found satisfactory.(I was not yet sassy enough to demand but, boy did I learn over the years that to get what the children or I might need I had to manipulate and omit many things that other men would have dealt with even if they would not have been in agreement)

His brother volunteered his pickup to help us move and he was just as lacking as Wence. The way they loaded the truck was so odd that two pieces of furniture flew off the back. The vacuum was totaled and a special piece of furniture that I had kept unblemished for over 20 years was badly gouged. I puddled up and both men declared," Hey it is only a piece of wood." I guess, but I was hurt at what I felt was a flippant and uncaring response.

Now we are settled in the larger house and the first argument we have is when he wants to tear up the entire back yard and turn it into garden area. No way man! Children need green spaces to play. Since he did not have a lawn or a yard when he was growing up, he could not understand my insistence on lawn. For heaven sake, you idiot woman kids can play in the dirt was certainly on his mind. He gave in and took only half of the yard for garden.

Play items were another thing he could not understand. I never had toys and I did fine was his lament. I would not relent and he finally set up a swing set, a tire tree, and a tunnel twenty feet long. These items got much use over the years as did a small trampoline and a rocking horse. At some later date he was able to say, I am glad you insisted (It sure would have been a lot easier if he had not made me jump through his goofy hoops first)

Wence continued his rotating shift at work and because it changed every seven days, the man was never tuned in to what was going on in the world or with his family. Because of the shift changes there were often times when he went as much as ten days without physically seeing his children. When I complained that he was not getting to know his children his comment was that it was up to the wife to rear the children. Excuse me? Who and what gave him that idea?

Laura had her first major earache at the age of ten months and Josef had pneumonia for the first time when he was ten months. I knew that there was a direct connection between the illnesses and Wence's smoking. When I asked if he could at least confine the smoking to one area in the house or at least open a window he snapped that he needed something to relax and that I better learn to deal with it. It took over 25 years before he actually understood the connection between smoking and respiratory problems. I guess, that is what you call a slow learner, huh?

I had grown up on a farm where hand work was a necessity and as a result I learned early on to read the signs of nature when things needed to be done. Work came first and we were often up with the dawn and at it until sundown. I was the row foreman by the time I started college. That meant I attended to the folks who were doing the handpicking of the crops while my sibs and mom attended to other things on the farm. I spent ten years in the classroom dealing with elementary age children. I felt that I had more than a reasonable knowledge of how behaviors worked. And yet, this man simply ignored me when I tried to explain what was appropriate for young children. I assumed that he was ignoring me but the reality was that he was not listening and therefore did not hear a thing I said. I should have caught onto that the day we brought Joe home from the hospital and he wanted to know if he could take his son hunting the following fall. A toddler? He most certainly did not have realistic expectations of what children were capable of at any age.

Since he had never been around small children, I excused a lot of the ignorance but as the children grew and his tolerance lessened then his coping skills could only work if he had managed to drink an excess of alcohol.

Not only did he have some strange ideas about the world, about children, and life in general, he had it in his head that HE had the only correct knowledge about all matters.

When we started out I thought that the reason for the numerous verbal mis-stepping was because English was not his mother tongue. Then I thought some more and came to the conclusion that since English was also spoken in the home this oddity had to be something else.

Could it be that he had some kind of hearing disorder? Could it be auditory dyslexia? Could that be the reason for what he told me was "baby talk" before he started school? The more I thought about all his little quirks the more confused I became. There had to be something else at work here. But what?

Rearing children by myself was such a full time job that his needs sort of fell by the wayside. Not only could I not be the wife he expected, I was not at all the subservient little mouse that his mother had been.

I guess for me, a former teacher, the most stressful part of this man was that he consistently mispronounced so many words. After a few attempts at correction and his irritation at my daring, I gave up that effort.

It was easier to ignore people who gave me the odd looks at his garbled words than it was to deal with his reaction.

1. He is in death up to his ears. (I have always wanted to ask, 'where is he from his ears up?') This has not changed in thirty-five years.

2. He owns me fifty dollars (Why does he 'own' you this money?) This man has never heard or understood the difference between owe and own. Confusing? Never to him!

Whenever there is a silent letter in a word, he makes a great effort to pronounce it and thus completely changes not only the sound but the meaning of the word.

3. He has never heard the difference between the letters M and
    N. Again, that makes for words of very different meaning.
    There are a good number of unvoiced letters in the English
language and he has consistently mixed up most of them There is
also a problem with the sound combination of "TH"

4. Adding syllables, reversing the order of any syllable in a word and
    taking away entire syllables has always made his speech unique.
    Why he does not hear the errors in his speech is anybody's
    guess but probably explains why he makes up his own words.
    A person's given name can be repeated several times over and
    he will still not be able to use it properly. Thus Tamara became
    Navarra(?) Juanita became Wanda and the list goes on...too
    numerous to list here.

5. Just recently he became angry with me when he asked where
    Monica lived. Since I know no one by that name I asked what
    he was talking about. He pitched out a wordy explanation and I
    was able to deduce that he meant Veronica. I pointedly said that
    her name was Veronica and he said, "What's the difference?"
    Quite a lot I would think, especially to Veronica.
    He refers to immediate family...my sibs and his by their given
names. He addresses women by their given names but he has never
called a male by anything except his surname. When asked why he
did not call men by the given name his response was that it made
him uncomfortable. I suspect it has something to do with the name
he was saddled with by his immigrant parents. His given name
taken from Czech history has ten letters and the middle name
is even worse. He endured so much teasing and humiliation over
the name that when he was a legal adult he seriously considered
changing it to something more Americanized.

Thus when our children came along we chose simple names that everyone could pronounce and did not lend themselves to cutesy nicknames.

Wife's job? What did that entail? Well since I was only an extension of him, that meant I was to do whatever he wanted and whenever he wanted. I was to be cook, housekeeper, cleaning lady, and spouse at all times. It was up to me to deal with all issues that did not relate to his job. Over time, I came to realize that he could not hold more than one thought in his head at any time. More would put him on overload that would erupt into arm chewing to the point of mutilation, pacing like a bull in a china shop, and generally bad mouthing the entire world.

During the second pregnancy he was, as my father would say, 'a busy little rooster.' He never considered my condition and since he was always more than a little intoxicated I learned to do a lot of faking. His ego blossomed, he would immediately roll over and be snoring before I could pull the covers up. I felt like a brood mare, ridden hard and put away wet. Years later he commented that he didn't understand how I could always climax when I was pregnant and never when I was not. That it might have something to do with his approach never entered his head and even today such consideration would be considered less than manly. If I complained of his roughness, he always shot back that there were plenty of women who would not gripe. Name me one I said and that conversation ended.

Without a doubt, I knew that there was a hidden depth in our children but Wence refused to notice. I talked to them as if they were just as ordinary as any other children. Wence preferred ignoring them or bad mouthing them in a very cruel way. Saying things such as they should have never been born, or that they were nothing but little animals was reason for me to puddle up and head for the laundry room where he could not see my tears. Years later Laura was able to repeat some of his nasty remarks and asked if dad really thought they were animals. That hurt more than I can say. When told of her comment dad denied that he ever had said such a thing. Long- term memory problems or just drunken babbling or hung over stupidity? I will probably never know.

As far as he was concerned Wence had done all he needed to do by fathering children. That he should be actively involved in the daily lives of his little ones just didn't compute. I would get down on the floor to play with them and he would ask why I did that. He could not understand that you needed to deal with children on their level.

Equating all life and that included manners down to a moral level was the only way his world made sense. Teaching table manners, and how to use eating utensils was a stupid exercise, he told me. What difference could it possibly make? How could I explain it to him so that it made sense to him? This from a man who regularly squatted in front of the fridge and ate with his fingers directly from the containers made me know that no matter how I might try he would not adjust his attitudes toward anything that was 'normal' to the rest of the world.

Manners were a constant festering annoyance to him and he saw no reason that being married and having a family should in any way change his behaviors. One incredibly annoying habit of his was to come to the stove and stick his fingers into whatever kettles I had on the stove. Just in recent time, I finally blew and when he put his fingers in the cooking pot I just happened to have a large slotted spoon in my hand. I whacked his hand with that and he let loose with unnecessary verbal barrage that would have had most women packing the bags and leaving. I finished cooking with no more taste attempts. However the next night there he was again. Just as he was reaching into the kettle, I let him see my spoon and he backed off. Why didn't I make that move a long time ago? Live and learn? I must be one heck of a slow learner too.

An older friend was always ready to listen when I found it necessary to vent my frustrations and was a real comfort. One thing that she commented was, "Why wouldn't he be aware just from being in the world? Surely, he would have learned by observation." And, that is the crux of the matter! Autism/Asperger's Syndrome folks are wandering the world as if they wear a blindfold. Explanation? These individuals are so into themselves and their egocentricity that for them the rest of the world ceases to exist. Their wants, needs, and desires are the only focus they understand. If the world does not respond in a way that is appropriate to their way of thinking then of course, the world is wrong.

Emotion is a concept that the man I married does not understand. One day he told me that he was "a cold bastard" and I could only stare at him. I was more than a little shocked that he would use that label even if it was and is true

One of the ways that I tried to teach the children respect for their father was to kiss him good night on the evenings when he was home. He never ever kissed them back but would pat each one on the head in such a way that years later Marie was able to tell me that he always gave her a headache when he did that. By the time Joe was two years old he insisted that he absolutely would not kiss the boy. When I objected he said ,"He's a boy" For Pete's sake, the kid was a toddler not a flaming homosexual. Did the man realize what he was implying? I doubt it

While he could not show emotion to either, me or his children, Wence was always willing to try to do things with them. One time we took the kids to fun center set up for the Rose Festival…what a crowd for small children to endure. Joe grabbed a plastic glass out of a young woman's hand and from the smell I knew it was beer. I was able to return the beer to her before the kid tasted it. Wence was so freaked out, that he insisted that we immediately leave. We did and I listened to a bad mouth litany all the way home. We will never be able to take them anywhere. Well golly gee, Joe was all of three years old! Didn't he have the ability to learn from his childish errors? Apparently not according to his father. We tried the fairway at the State Fair later in the summer and another Joe incident occurred. We were walking along when Joe grabbed an ice cream cone out of the hand of a young teenaged girl. That boyfriend swung around with his fist up but I was able to return the cone before Joe tasted it. Again Wence was totally freaked and insisted that we leave immediately. To satisfy him we did so. On the way home, he made it very clear that he would never take them anywhere again. (So, it became more and more obvious that the man had no understanding of child development.) If he had, neither of these episodes would have been so devastating to him.

It was then up to me to see that the children learned to be in and a part of the world that this man simply did not understand. By the time Marie was two years old I was taking all three of them to church on Sunday on a fairly regular basis. We sat in front near the choir and that music kept them on their best behavior. After the service people would remark on how well all three of them behaved.

Wence continued to be totally committed to his job and had no time to support me or the children and so he became a sort of useless appendage. The children and I did our thing and he did his without any thought as to what we might like from him, and he never ever thought to ask

The stress of house payment, home maintainence, medical issues, and family just drew him into himself to such a degree that talking to him was like talking to myself. He looked like he was listening and when questioned later would have no memory of the conversation. I soon realized that he had never heard me at all.

The only way he could cope with life was to self medicate with his home- made wine. He made wine out of everything from dandelions to raspberries to plums and apples. It was not unusual for him to put nearly a gallon a night in his stomach. Marie was so aware of this that by the time she was a first grader it was not uncommon for her to ask if we could get a divorce. When asked why she thought we should she commented that she hated him when he was a slobbering drunk That he was drunk by the third glass and more often than not had trouble finding his way to bed became a constant In the beginning, I would sit with him and try to have an adult conversation. Then I thought, why am I doing this? After the children were tucked in bed for the evening, I would stay with him perhaps for less than an hour and get myself off to bed for the children were early risers

He would stumble his way to bed and sometime the stumbling landed him on the floor. Rather than try to lift him I would throw a blanket over him and leave him on the floor. I cannot count the number of times he emptied himself on the carpet. Of course, the odor according to him was natural so I was not to do anything about it. Is it any wonder that my sibs and my parents did not want to stop in for a visit? He did not and, has never understood why no one did. Would you want to step into a house that constantly smelled like a urinal and rotten eggs?

The alcoholic intake meant that libido increased . If I was already asleep he would wake me and try his level best to insert that flimsy strip of a wet noodle. It never worked and it was always my fault. One particular night I was sleeping so soundly that I pulled away when he came in That earned me a hard swat on the fanny and his comment, "You are my wife dammit.' Reluctantly I accepted his efforts but would not make eye contact the next day. After 24 hours, he did manage a half -hearted apology. He could be so very involved in his attempts at intimacy and yet if he heard a car door slam outside or a dog barking in the distance or a siren down the street he would immediately collapse.

Since intimacy was so unkind to me I was somewhat relieved when at the age of forty, he declared, "We are too old for sex" and then added,

Well maybe once in awhile. Once in awhile became less and less and I can honestly say that I have never felt that I have missed out on anything precious. The idea of any other kind of intimacy was in the dumpster too. A quick kiss, a back rub, holding hands, a touch in passing were all put in the same category as no sex. Life early on in this marriage became an emotional vacuum. I could have stayed in the convent for all the intimacy that, was offered, in this marriage

Before moving to another subject this must be noted. In spite of his inabilities in the bedroom he thought he was hot stuff' and one night asked, "Did you just have an organism? NOT and before I could control it I burst into laughter. "Did you mean orgasm?" "Isn't that what I just said?" Boy did that laughter deflate his ego.

The lesson I learned was let him have his illusions/delusions (He wasn't about to make any effort at improvement or change.)

Stresses of everyday life were more than this man could handle. He had been gainfully employed at the same place for well over twenty years when there was a change in the way things were being done. A new, younger boss was put in charge and Wence would come home in a rage almost every shift. He thought that his college degree put him head and shoulders above the crowd when it came to abilities. Extended degrees mean nothing in the scheme of things if you don't have a clue about social values. All I could say to him was that since it was the boss speaking he had better listen even if he did not agree with what was being said

So often, this man made statements that were so off the wall that even the most simple minded soul would suspect that something was not quite right

One evening when the children had been tucked in bed I sat down in the living room rocking chair. He was already on the sofa watching television. He said that he was really tired and I commented that so as I

He shot back, "Why, you don't work. Since I had just canned fruit that day around the chores of looking after the children who were all in diapers, and washing in the old wringer machine, I simply stared at him without comment. My expression must have said more than I could have voiced because he immediately blushed. Of course, taking care of children and lugging wet laundry up the stairs to the clothes lines was not work at all.

Wence was so programmed to believe that the wife took care of the house the children, the budget, the medicals and whatever else surfaced that the more I did the more he expected. The intensity with which he approached every task was enough to make me terribly uncomfortable. When he would search for a missing penny as he reconciled the bank account like it was spun gold I was more than willing to take over the budget management. That was the appropriate thing for me to do because this man had no idea of what it cost to maintain a house or the appropriate nutrition for small children. We had more than one disagreement on that matter. He presumed that if he liked something than it was an automatic given that the children would also like it. While Laura was still a toddler he started slicing pieces of his snack of raw onion and sharing that with her. As a result, today Laura will choose an onion over a piece of cookie or an apple. In fact, her intestinal tract very much acts like Wence's. I have yet to break her of sneaking an onion into her room to munch on at night. When I have complained the daddy thinks it is highly amusing.

He loves to chew/gnaw on meat bones…the kind that the butcher would probably throw in the garbage. His meat of preference is ribs and the closer to raw the better. That his small children who were not yet school age did not have the teeth for this stuff totally befuddled him. If they did not like what he liked then I must be training them the wrong way. Nor could he understand that small children were normally not capable of digesting raw vegetables. Cabbage leaves, kale, and Brussels sprouts according to him were to be eaten raw. No matter how I tried HE was always nutritionally correct and I was wrong. Eating raw meat got to be such a problem that I enlisted the aid of others to get him to stop that less than healthful habit. All in all ,it took over 20 years before he stopped that practice

Wence, from what he has told me , had an inadequate diet growing up and so it has left some strange attitudes about food. When we were first married I cooked as my mother had…making enough of the evening meal to have some left overs for the next day at noon. Left over food was to be eaten I soon learned. He would clean out the fridge of all left over food before the night was gone. I was always amazed at the capacity of his appetite. He could sit to a table with any three men and eat as much food by himself as the other three combined. This quirk has never changed. I tried to keep a well stocked refrigerator but he made such a habit of going there for no good reason that I would find it necessary to restock the shelves at least twice a week. There are pictures in my album of this man squatting in front of the fridge eating directly out of the containers with his fingers. (fingers came before spoons didn't they?) In all of the time we have been married I can not honestly remember that Wence has ever eaten off a dinner plate. A cereal bowl is his preference for breakfast lunch and dinner. He has perfected the art of stacking his entire meal in the bowl in such a way that I have never seen him spill anything out of the dish. A cup or glass was always a chance to spill something Using a fork and knife is too much of a chore and so he uses a spoon only. Whenever I have made even a minor issue of his less than laudable eating habits he has always snapped that I am too concerned with what people might say. Not at all but if our children see how he addresses food issues then can I expect them not to imitate him?

Having grown up in a close knit large family, any holiday was a good enough reason for us to gather to celebrate and to stay connected. When we married it was a given that we would be hosts for some of these events. Wence thought it was a marvelous idea that his in-laws were such a close family. My mother gathered the family at her home for Christmas, my sister had everyone for Easter celebrations and I was designated to be the Thanksgiving host. This worked fine for about five years and then Wence began to complain that this stuff was a bunch of garbage…because he would have to wait (perhaps) an extra hour or so for the main meal of that day. Now since he was not in any immediate danger of dying from hunger pangs I ignored as much as I could. Oh he was polite enough when all the people were here. As soon as the guests were gone he would start the negative monologue. An hour or two would have been sufficient for me to get his message but it would continue for days. It served absolutely no purpose but to irritate me Finally I made it clear to my mom and sis that I simply could no longer deal with Wence's attitude and would have to discontinue the Thanksgiving gathering. They thought there was definitely something wrong with the man but agreed to abide by my decision. Because he had made such an issue, they agreed that it would be wisest to cancel the Christmas and Easter gatherings too. It made me sad because that was cutting us off from an important family and social connection but he was vastly relieved. He was soooo glad so I buried my sadness and moved on as best I could.

Not only were holidays reason for cranky negative discourses on the stupidity of such celebrations, birthdays and anniversary dates received the same negative verbalizations. Now since I wanted my children to have 'normal' experiences and I knew he would put a kink in any attempts, I would focus on a small celebration for each child when he was on a swing shift. I seriously doubt that he ever had any idea of what was happening. He never remembered his own birthday unless someone mentioned it and he certainly never remembered mine and after the first year he no longer remembered our anniversary. If asked today he could not give either the correct date or year. And if asked his children's birthdays or ages he would be hard put to come up with a correct answer. Normal male behavior? I don't think so. Sad? You bet it is because he does not realize or even care that he is missing so much.

Well then you might ask, "What about Christmas?" The most major holiday in the Christian world was downgraded to just another day by Wence. Why? I most certainly do not understand, but I suspect it is because he truly does not understand the essence of what the Christmas celebration is . Trying to explain that to him was like talking to a wall. Wence is not dim witted but sometimes I had to wonder. To him the holiday did not make sense. Gift giving was not to be tolerated and decorations of any kind were dismissed as 'more garbage.' He simply could not understand the concept of gift giving and was seriously pissed if he received a gift from anyone on any occasion.

This negative attitude about holidays had an effect on the children. After about twenty five years had passed and nothing had changed I asked the children what they wanted to do for the holiday. My son said , "Let's not do anything.' Why did he feel that way I had to ask. His response was that ' dad always really mad about Christmas.. it just doesn't feel nice. So let's not. Dad be better then.' The girls agreed and that was the end of Christmas in this house For the last 10 years there have been no decorations, no tree, no Nativity set and no gifts. I did manage to buy one gift apiece and see that it is given to each person when Wence is not around. The children certainly seem to understand him better than he has ever understood them. It has always been a stress situation for them and rather than walk on eggshells to keep him happy, it has been easier on them too to let him dictate everything that happens in this house

Being connected to the Church community was an integral part of our family life when I was growing up. As our children came along, I expected this pattern to continue. One of the first things I did toward that end was to start teaching them prayers. Angel of God, my guardian dear was the first one I started with. When Wence became aware that I was doing this he told me that I was really being…well I won't repeat what he thought. They don't know what you are talking about he told me. I knew better and so prayer times were moved to the children's rooms. As they grew older I added more of the Christian litany of common prayers and by the time they were all school age, we had about twenty minutes worth of prayer time each night.

By the time children reached school age and I knew that they would not attend a regular school, I approached our pastor about religious classes for the developmentally delayed. He was not comfortable with my questions and referred me to the diocesan office. From that place I was eventually contacted by the office for people with disabilities. Within a short time there was a program established for this group of children. One evening a week they participated in a religious class for two hours. The ladies who ran the class were volunteers of a special kind. They accepted each child fully as a child of God. It was wonderful for the children.

That summer there was a preparation class every Sunday afternoon for a larger group who were ready to participate in the sacramental liturgy. By the end of summer this young group were ready and Wence refused to come to that service. I have to work he said but that was such a lame excuse. There would have been no problem if he had asked for time off. The reality is that this was not important to him so obviously it could not be important to his children. Repeatedly, he told me that they had no idea what was going on. With the passage of time, it has become apparent that the children have a rich spiritual life beyond anything I can explain and most certainly beyond Wence's ability to understand. There is a deep sadness here that he does not believe his children capable of spiritual understanding.

Whomever it was that coined the term obsessive compulsive, must have had Wence in mind. This man has yet to do anything spontaneously. He must think, discuss, digest and wonder if he has made the correct choice. He will travel twenty miles or more to check, whether or not he remembered to turn off a coffee pot. He has established patterns that must be followed to the letter. Example 1. Every Sunday he goes to the group home to visit our son. He will sit and discuss what he is going to do when he gets to the group home. He always leaves at three o'clock in the afternoon. It has been seven years and he never has deviated….it is never two forty-five or three fifteen. Predictable beyond a doubt as he can not tolerate any deviation from his decisions.

Example two… The pattern in his life when he gets up in the morning is always the same, the bathroom, his floor exercises to keep his back flexible, and then back to the bedroom to dress. Now that is a major undertaking . I have purposely timed this process and over time nothing has changed. He takes thirty- nine minutes to pull on a pair of trousers and slip into shoes and sox. Never thirty eight or forty minutes. This has never wavered from that time slot.

Such utter predictability was making me crazy because he could not bend. To keep my sanity I made it a point to keep myself in bed with my back turned to him. To this day I still do that and he has never been aware that I am always awake and attuned to his pokiness.

Once when I asked him why he repeated himself so much he replied that he wanted to make sure he was understood. In general, most people get the message after a couple repetitions and maybe a couple questions. This man however has been known to stay on a subject for as long as there is daylight and then began the process all over on the next day.

Our children caught on early, and if dad was in one of his constant repeating episodes, all three of them would move to their bedrooms It is doubtful that he ever understood that they were trying to get away from him Constant repetition and a set pattern to every hour of his day and absolutely no flexibility about anything has to be an obsession

Since he had so little in the way of material goods and necessities growing up, he has become the classic rat packer. He does not care much about clothes items but he sure collects a lot of other junk. He is in his seventh heaven when he can go to the Goodwill as is and bring home all kinds of things for which he has no earthly use. This is a facility that is the last stop for recycled items before they are sent to landfill. Items are such poor shape, that stuff is sold by the pound. Has he ever brought home anything useful? Not once and he goes to that place at least once every two weeks. He is literally filling our house with junk. And, I have to wait for when he will decide that the original kitchen and bathroom of this house are in need of replacement. Probably not in my lifetime or at least not as long as he is alive.

Since he grew up in such a dysfunctional environment it is hard for me to understand why he thinks this is an ideal for which his children should reach. Excuse me? Why is this an ideal? No indoor plumbing, no electricity, and no running water in the house is not my notion of ideal. He has mentioned in passing that he does not ever remember his dad taking a bath and never ever saw him wash his hands. An aunt told me that she never ever saw her brother in law in clean clothes; that they were always so dirty that they could have probably stood by themselves. Maybe the fact that I have a hard time getting this man to wear clean clothes regularly stems from the fact that his father did not. Having had so little in material goods has left some strange life attitudes. in Wence's brain One time on a walk down the bicycle trail he came across 3 pairs of boxer underwear that he picked up and brought home. He insisted that they would fit him and wanted to put them in his drawer at once. Not until I had sent those things through two bleach washes without any other items in the wash would I allow him to put them in his drawer. He has picked up and brought home all kinds of inappropriate items…broken pens, torn papers, crushed up receipts and even once a used condom. Now that condom did cause me to do a fair amount of yelling at his stupidity. That made me a cantankerous bitch! By his standard of course!

After his brother passed away, the neighbors told the wife that this had been a very strange family. Many neighbors had to use the rutted road in front of the home and it was noted that if the parents were outdoors when they heard a vehicle approaching, they would rapidly disappear behind the buildings. The consensus seemed to be that they were so shy they didn't know how to deal with people. True? Probably in some degree and that could explain why Wence would run to hide under the kitchen stove whenever there was a knock on the door. He would not emerge until the visitor left. While as a youngster he exhibited a degree of shyness his brother was just the opposite. So there was a constant clash between the two brothers.

In his adult years, he realized that some of the testing he was put through as a child was actually attempts to see whether or not he might be retarded. The fact that he did so poorly in school was not that he was stupid, but that his sensory system was on overload. Too many farm kids brought the farm smells into the classroom. Not that Wence was a clean freak, but he never smelled himself. He was just as ripe as the rest of them. School was only a place to be, not a place to learn life skills until he was nearing the end of high school. The possibility of college reared its head and then he began to put serious effort into study. There was no way that his elderly parents could even help with college. So he joined the Marines with the specific intention of using the G.I bill to put himself through school. He served his time and then enrolled in a private college out of state. He was accepted on probation and proved himself, by the end of the first semester. He graduated, with a degree in Business. He worked at varying jobs with that degree but did not like sitting at a desk. He eventually wound up working in a factory that made glass containers of all sorts and had a fairly strong union. He stayed at that place for over thirty years and cannot understand that today that is not a norm for folks. Can you imagine today's generation staying at one job for the entire work life?

I realize that some of this sounds as if I am purposely making this man sound like a total misfit but that is not my intention. More than anything I want people who read this to realize that the eccentricity that drives my spouse is deep seated and unchangeable. and autistic

It is known that over forty percent of the autistic population is sound sensitive and I am convinced that this is one of Wence's major problems. Somewhere in his distant past, in order to cope with sensory overload, he learned to tune out the world to such a degree that he is no longer aware of all the beauty that is out there. He can appreciate beauty when he so chooses but prefers the mundane. One time he told me that mucking around in the manure pile in the family barn was a pure delight when he was growing up. Was that a kinesthetic experience? Maybe, because so many things that involve touch and feel are still strange to him today. He has a very tough skin and yet his phobia about needles is funny. I have seen him near fainting from a needle prick. I have also seen him ignore an overly large sliver that was badly infected. He hadn't even been aware.

No one in this house likes the music that has surfaced in the last twenty five years. The children and I are great fans of classical music and while Wence does not object to our listening to it he regularly tells us that it is not perky enough.

He approves of the 1812 Overture and the Overture from Carmen. And he does accept Gregorian Chant…probably because that was the church music he grew up with. It is known that chant can soothe overexcited brain waves enough to calm an out of control individual

Asperger/autism (A/A) people if examined closely are very narcissistic. The world is all about ME. ME ME. That is not to say that these individuals are not intelligent. In fact of all the DD population they are probably closest to the so called 'normal Bell curve.' Superior intelligence does not matter in the least if one can not deal with the realities of the world. The biggest issue for my spouse is that he thinks he is the only person in the world who has the correct spin on all things that happen in this world. He can rant about morals, crooked politicians, global warming, overpaid public employees, obnoxious cashiers, the price of gasoline, repairmen who are basically gougers, the disarray in the public schools, the lawyers who pick on Catholics or Catholic doctrine and on and on.

Where does that put me? Right in the middle of discussions that drive me more than a little bit nuts. I get so tired of his superior attitude about all things. He has never taken a vehicle to a repair shop because all mechanics are crooks. People are being gouged by the current price of gasoline. All politicians are liars. All public employees are overpaid. (Having been a classroom teacher before marriage certainly never led me to that conclusion). This house is falling down around our ears because there has not been an update since it was built in 1952, but I refuse to let him try any repair because when he replaced a bathroom floor several years ago he left a mess that took me a week to clean up. To this day I will never understand how he got linoleum glue inside the tub. Do you know how hard that stuff is to get up? Do you wonder why I say no to any effort he offers? Anything he has ever repaired was only ever done half way. Recently he had to replace a sink that had rusted out. He went out and came back with a sink from a junk store. I was terribly upset that we didn't rate more than a ten dollar piece of junk. He was totally confused and asked ,"You wanted a new one?" Well of course you self centered oddity. A new one is easier to clean. This thing he installed is badly pitted, extremely hard to keep clean and has a lot of permanent stains. His comment was so what if there are stains. These kinds of happenings have come down the pike so often that I simply don't try anymore. That way I have better control of my emotions and he does not even try to understand how I feel

Wence is a gossip and claims he is only interested in what is good about the neighbors. Not true! After he gets the gossip, he comes home and bad mouths everyone of them. I was always taught that if you can't say something nice about someone or something then don't say anything at all. Wence tends to embellish all that gossip with his own spin on it which is never what the reality is. Usually I have already heard the gossip and choose not to pass it along.

A particularly annoying habit he has is to stand by his pickup and gawk around the neighborhood. Gawk is the word that best fits this habit and several neighbors and his own daughter have commented that this gawking makes him look retarded. I have chided him for this and he claims that he is only gazing around to make sure the neighborhood is safe. Since he has no real awareness level that statement is amusing.

One of the soothing things that appealed to the children was to go riding in the car if Wence was not along. On one occasion after there had been a near miss when he was driving the car, the kids wanted to talk about how frightened they had been. Somehow the car seemed to encourage confidences and they all three mentioned how dad never looks at the road but always looks to the side. I was astounded to realize that they were that tuned in and knowing that this was a safety issue, I soon learned to take over the majority of driving tasks if the family was involved. He was given the option of joining us or staying home. Mostly he chose to stay home and the ride was a relaxing time away from the worst back seat driver and screecher that I have ever known

Wence has never given a straight yes or no answer to anything. Every word, every sentence needs a qualifier. In recent time he was asked to fill out a questionnaire in which one question asked if he used alcohol of any kind. 'I do not' he said and I called him a liar. I told him that he was chronically hung over for his entire work life, and short tempered all the time so that definitely says he uses alcohol in excess. By all definitions, this man is an alcoholic and yet he has been in denial our entire marriage. Time after time, I have been with him when that kind of question has been asked. He denies it every time and it is only out of marital respect that I don't call him on his denials in front of others. It would only add more ice to an already emotionless relationship.

One very strange thing that caregivers in the autism community have discovered is that there is almost a universal paranoia about the body organs among some of this population. Wence has always been obsessed with the workings of his bowels. He routinely reports to me how many times a day he has a bowel movement and relates its size, color and texture. Why he does this, I have no idea. Maybe it is part and parcel of his childish bathroom humor. What he considers to be uproariously funny is just plain bad taste and I cannot be amused by it.

When we were first married, he only bathed twice a week. Since he worked in a factory in a very dirty job, I told him a daily bath was an absolute if he expected me to sleep in his bed. He owned 4 pairs of underclothes and all in stained white. One of the first things I insisted on was more boxers, and he was astounded to find out that one could buy colored tee shirts. I insisted on a few more shirts and trousers too as he only had two sets. He was adamant that he would never wear jeans and I honored that .He also insisted that his children would never wear jeans. I got around that by buying jeans in other colors than denim. He never knew the difference.

One of the first medical procedures I insisted on was dental care. I sent him for a check-up which the dentist did and then told him that he could not be his dentist for any thing else. Why? He looked Wence in the eye and told him that in five years his teeth would be falling out and he didn't want to be the one blamed. Turned out the man was right. One by one Wence's upper set of teeth began falling out. When he had lost six he finally agreed to go to a dentist. Two more fell out and the dentist suggested an upper plate. Of course that meant putting out money and he could not make up his mind. After several weeks of should I or shouldn't I he finally agreed. His partial denture serves him well and he takes careful care of it. Before the partial, tooth brushing was a hit and miss affair. Now he brushes twice a day.

I really wish he would give the same consideration to his personal hygiene. Once he retired from work, he reverted to the old habit of twice a week bathing. Every day could be so much better but he says he doesn't care if others find him offensive. I have seen people's eyebrows go up when he walks by. His body odor could choke an elephant. Part of this is due, I think, to the fact that he lives for the taste of garlic. A day without garlic is like a day without sunlight. He can not function if he does not have at least one entire bulb each day, not just a clove or two but an entire bulb along with at least one onion. He has been doing this for so many years that the smell oozes from his skin. The smell of sulfur in this house is such a constant that the rest of the family has learned to live with it but visitors to the house have been mentioning for the last thirty years how strongly this place smells of sulfur and Wence.

Anything with a strong garlic component, such as garlic soup gets high marks from Wence. Any item grown by him in his garden is the best possible produce. His way is the best way and even if it were proven to him in black and white on writing paper, that there are other equally adequate ways to grow tomatoes he would not believe or approve of any other way but his. The idea of training the vines from cucumber, squash, melon and pumpkin is something he has never done even though I have been harping for years that such an endeavor would give him better control of the harvest. Since it was not his own thought there was no way that he could accept that his farm reared wife might possibly have a valid idea.

Because he is the master authority on all things, I have never been able to maintain any kind of flower gardens that he didn't destroy. More than once I have planted some sort of flower and the next thing I knew, he had torn it out. And always the reasoning was that he didn't know it was a flower. If it is in a flower garden wouldn't you assume it was a flower? So he didn't know (not an uncommon problem for him about so many things) but wouldn't most ordinary folks come and ask?

His peasant roots surface every time there is even a tiny square of soil available for planting. To leave that spot bare would be unthinkable and I have to really grouse at him to be sure that he will leave it alone.

Seedlings that are volunteers from the previous year are not to be touched…unless I get them pulled before he notices them. Even if the seedlings are non producers they must be nurtured. So that time spent in garden pursuits does keep him out of my hair.

He planted a couple fennel plants that took over the area where they were seeded. He has enough fennel in jars to last the next fifty years and yet he had to have more. The current crop is drying and he will have an additional fifty years worth for his taste buds. If I can ever get him out of the house for a day there is a lot of junk plants that will die a painless death since they serve no reasonable purpose but for the fact that he was able to grow them.

This tends to be the same situation with his fruit trees; a plum tree that is usually so loaded that the branches break and the leaves curl; an apple tree with so many varieties planted on it and branches wandering twenty feet from the trunk at eye level;a plum seedling so close to the edge of the cement that it will either break the cement or have to be removed. It WILL not be removed in his lifetime. The grapes and pears are another foolish situation. We have always had more than enough pears from one tree but he got it in his head that we needed more variety and so has planted two more trees that will never mature in his lifetime. When we started with the original grapes he wanted so many more but I was able to stop him at a dozen plants. He has never realized that all this stuff he planted would someday produce beyond his expectations. HE does not believe in using chemicals so we have buckets and buckets of wormy, inedible fruits and what the bugs don't get to first the squirrels find delectable.

Kale and cabbage rank right up there with garlic as prime vegetables. The only garden items that interest the rest of the family would be the beets and carrots. We like the cucumbers and tomatoes too but as a matter of survival we tend to ignore much of that simply because of his obsession with this stuff. Wence tries to force us into eating when we don't want or need it.

What kind of guy is this? You may ask yourself if he is normal by the world's definition. He definitely is not.

Back to personal hygiene for a minute. Wence gasses out liberally and since it always has a strong sulfur component and he has never been able to cleanse adequately, his clothing has a chronic smell that is not pleasant. Trying to get him to put on clean clothes and under things was always a major undertaking. As a result, the chair he always sits on (and there is only one that he sits on) developed its own unique odor. There is also the chronic staining because he sits around in his boxers with no thought to the marks he might be leaving. I finally got smart and invested in the chair cushions used in kitchens and put them where he sat. After a few weeks I could throw those away rather than drive myself mad by trying to keep the furniture clean. Recently, I had to do the cleaning chore because he managed to leave his mark (just like a dog marking his territory) on a chair. When he discovered that the chair seat had no marks he was soooo upset. I scolded him for that kind of remark and he whined, "But that was MY chair." Did that mean I should not see that it looked like normal people sat in it? If I was embarrassed by the stains then that was not his fault and I was caring about things that did not and do not matter. Isn't this man a real gem?

To empty his bladder has always resulted in spray on the walls, drippings down the front of his trousers and a long crystallized stain down the toilet bowl to the floor that requires me to get down on my stomach on a regular basis with a razor to get that muck off. I am sincerely hoping that I do not have to clean his toilet bowl when we get to Heaven. In an ideal world, Wence would have his own toilet that no one else would need to share. Maybe then he wouldn't need to vocalize with such sincere pain as if something were dramatically wrong. When asked if there was something amiss his response is always that 'relief feels so good.'

He can grouse and grumble like a river boat gambler when he needs the bathroom and someone else is in there. The verbal abuse he dishes out on such occasions would have most women leaving him in the dust. Because he does not have the ability to wait, he has made a habit of going out to the backyard to do his thing. There is a permanent odd odor in the patio area he uses. Even though I use gallons of Purex on a regular basis the odor remains.

It is bad enough that he openly uses the backyard to pee but it is entirely inexcusable that he comes back in with his fly undone and his boxers open to anyone's view. Marie has enough sass that every so often when he sits in his chair in that condition she will snap, "For Pete sake, Dad. No one wants to look at THAT." Her tone is usually enough to make him stand and zip himself…at least until the next time he has to relieve himself. I have to observe him before he leaves the house to make sure that he has remembered to zip himself. For whatever reason, going unzipped in public does not seem to concern him. I refuse to go with him when he is in that condition and he thinks I am an unreasonable prude. Personal pride does not seem to be on his screen of awareness

Whether this man is a classic A/A individual or just some kind of genetic anomaly I have never figured. He has so many traits shared by that population and yet so many other traits that are unique to him.

Not too long ago a person who has been involved in the analysis of handwriting characteristics for over thirty years took an interest in Wence's written words. I do know that this is not an exact science but she hit the nail on the head with such accuracy that it was almost scary.

Self-centered, egotistical, cruel, cold, and unwilling to share anything about himself. Those were just the first reactions. His attitudes about life center around ME…ME…ME. That jibes with what his closest and oldest friend told me. As long as he has known this man his friend says that he has always been the most stubborn, opinionated and arrogant person he has ever known. Not much of a recommendation to get along in the world is it?

Does the fact that Wence is so into himself explain why I can stand shoulder to shoulder with him and he is not aware that I am there? He can hold only one thing in his mind at a time. Many times he has really lost his cool if I give him a "Honey do list" that is more than two items long.

We all know that every wife and mother has her own to do list that is probably as long as her arm

While I have been noting that this man was really not a good husband other than handing over his paycheck so he could crawl in his wine bottle, he was definitely not a good father at all. His responsibility ended at conception. I suspect that he does not know anything intimately about any of his children. Marie has pretty much tuned him out because at the age of thirty one he is still treating her like a five year old. He complains that she has no friends and then when she does bring someone to the house he rejects them as losers and tells her to get rid of that jerk be it male or female. And he wonders why she avoids him and spends most of her time in her room? Honestly I don't blame her.

When she was fifteen he took Marie out for her first driving lesson and they were back home in less than ten minutes. She was sobbing and shaking so badly she could hardly walk. Wence was right behind her ranting and raving like a lunatic about what a rotten driver she was. In less than ten minutes? How could he possibly know that? Did he ever explain her error? No he didn't… she was supposed to automatically know what she had done wrong. She saved her money and hired a regular driving trainer who gave her twelve lessons and said that she had the potential to be an excellent driver. Fifteen years have passed and Wence still harps on what a lousy driver she is. Within this past year she did have an accident that was her fault and he is still harping about it. Finally I told him that since he was in the insurance risk pool for the serious accidents that he had before we were married he had no business bad mouthing Marie for one accident in fifteen years. He huffed and buffed up his 'halo' and declared that he never had any accident that was his fault except when he was drunk. So he, therefore, is beyond criticism. What a guy!

Marie has always been a good student and been on the honor roll regularly since fourth grade. Whenever that was pointed out to her dad he would say, "that 's good Marie but don't get a swelled head.' Is it any wonder that her self esteem is essentially in the toilet? Every positive compliment was and is always followed by a negative one so that she began to say. "Why try?" That comment always made me sad and my heart aches for her and what kinds of potential her father's tirades have destroyed.

The women on both sides of this family are amply endowed and so both of our girls were gifted with more than ample bosoms. Growing up in a rural environment as a young girl, I was not too bothered by that but was more than a little surprised at what the girls had to go through living in a large city. By the time she was sixteen Marie was begging for breast reduction and I was more than willing because replacing a bra every month was becoming an expensive routine. At age eighteen I took her to a surgeon who said yes reduction was necessary. The insurance company gave approval and Wence had a fit. Finally, he called the moral ethicist at the local Catholic hospital who said that such procedure was acceptable because it would put her on parity with women of normal breast size. And it did! The ribald comments, the bus stalkers the entire messy scenario came to a halt. She was dumbfounded that people, women included started to make eye contact. And, there was a major change in her personality. Too bad the dad always makes us jump through unwanted hoops

When it was determined that Joe and Laura were seriously autistic their father simply shut down and withdrew from active family life, becoming more of a fixture than an active participant. I got them started in special education by the time Laura was three. There was an expectation of parental involvement and Wence vigorously objected to his part. It was always…"You go and then tell me" I did go and I did tell him but it didn't take long for me to realize that he was not even hearing my reports so I stopped that endeavor. I stayed actively involved in the parental advisory committees all the way through the education years and when I told him I was really getting tired his response was that if I didn't stay involved who would?

On one occasion when we were invited as a family to dinner at my parents Wence had just come off graveyard and was somewhat less than rational. We filed into the house and Laura accidentally stepped on the back of his shoe. He swung around with his fist up and actually hit her in the abdomen…not as hard as he could have when he realized what he was doing but still enough to hurt and to make Laura very leery of being anywhere in his vicinity for a long time. My dad saw the whole episode and let it be known that he did not think much of a guy who would hit a small child. I also let my spouse know that I thought he showed less than adult behavior. He never apologized to Laura and was more concerned that his father-in-law thought he was a jerk. I am really not a bad guy he told me and I told him to convince his father-in-law. I was becoming tired of him always excusing his behavior because he was not 'aware.'

Excuses! Always excuses and the constant refrain that he was not aware just did not sit well with me because he was forever pointing out how well educated, and well spoken he was. Again, out of respect, I did not point out that he could not carry on a conversation in a group or even one on one without a great deal of stuttering. If you did not know this man it would be easy to assume from all the incomplete sentences that he really might be retarded. He cannot take messages or instructions over the phone. I got smart and had a message voice mail put on the phone. He was told not to pick up the phone. If it was for him we would call him to the phone

Complicated sentences confuse him. Simple sentence structure is a must and even then there may be difficulty. Driving from point A to point B can not be done without a navigator in the car, especially if it is to an area he is not familiar with. Even then, the navigator patience can be tried beyond belief, because everything must be repeated and repeated in order for anything to register in that brain. On occasion he has been given very simple 1-2-3-written instructions on how to find an address and he still can get lost. In fact he does this on a regular basis and then comes home and gripes in spades about how inaccurate the information was. Autism or early dementia? At this point we don't know.

Years and years of daily alcohol consumption in excess of what would be considered a relaxing amount, seem to have affected Wence's memory very badly. Many of the things that the children did as small fry were being reviewed a few days ago and he told me that he does not remember any of it. I was not shocked but I was certainly saddened to know that he was so removed from his children even if he was physically present. He no longer seems to need so much of the delusional comfort of alcohol He does continue to deny that he ever drank in excess. I have finally learned to let it be because he will always be in denial.

Wence seems to have this sense of how well spoken and polished he is just because he got himself a college degree. The truth is that he suffers from 'potty mouth syndrome.' What is that? ... A husband and father who thinks there is nothing wrong with using foul language and four letter words. He broke himself of using SOB when Marie repeated his identical words at the age of two. However all the other vulgar language has been part and parcel of who he is from the very start of our marriage. Over and over, I have asked him to clean up his mouth and he is adamant that there is nothing wrong with vulgarity. Then my response has to be, 'you call this polished and well spoken?" He does not like to hear that but I keep hoping that if I say it often enough he will get the idea that truly refined people do not use vulgarity as an integral part of their vocabulary. Am I fighting a losing battle? Probably because I think the vulgarity is part and parcel of undiagnosed Tourette's Syndrome.

Other odd vocal habits include using the word 'what' at the end of every sentence. Does that require a response? Yes, even a growl seems to be sufficient because if I do not respond, then he keeps repeating. 'what?" The most annoying oddity is when he uses my given name as a punctuation mark Add all the other odd vocalizations that make absolutely no sense, humming, sighing, grunting, groaning, and undignified snorting and it has to be Tourettes. He can not come into a room and begin any kind of conversation without all these manifestations, and 'shit, hell, damn' being the beginning structure of every sentence he utters. If I respond to any of this, he will say, "oh nothing"

Awareness of the environment is basic to most human interaction…at least that has always been how I thought the world worked. With Wence in my life the meaning of that word took on an entirely new reality. Driving in the country side was always an enjoyable experience until the kids came along and I would point out things to them and then comment to Wence and invariably his response was, 'I wasn't aware.' For a man who claimed to be critically aware of his world that comment always confused me. The reality was that Wence only THOUGHT he was aware. We had so many near misses with other cars that I soon put a stop to family drives because it upset everyone, but Wence, so badly. I am a good driver became a tired refrain. Why were the near misses always the fault of the other driver? And being a constant back seat driver drove Marie and me both nuts. I can't begin to count how many times one of his screeching episodes caused whichever one of us was driving to hit the brakes; only to hear him say, 'O nothing you can keep going,' This was such an constant and so not needed that finally in the past year after one of his episodes I commented that I really wanted to stop the car and slap him upside the head. Laura was in the front seat and wore this goofy grin all the way home. I must have made an impression because the back seat driving is at an all time low. I can hear him starting to say something and then he chokes it back. I suspect that learning to be quiet is hard for him, but a safer option for all of us.

On one occasion I put new curtains on the kitchen widows and the children spotted them as soon as they were in the door from school. I praised them for noticing and assumed Wence would also notice. Since he did not I decided to wait and see how long before he would notice. Time slipped by and at the end of the eight month I asked if he liked the new curtains. Why was I surprised when he admitted that he had not noticed? And, he called himself 'very aware!' Hah!

Josef has suffered from idiopathic epilepsy since the age of eight and as he grew the frequency of attacks were unpredictable. We tried to keep his environment as safe as possible and that meant a padded rocking chair was his favorite place to sit. It was a Saturday summer night and I decided to go to church services. I told Wence he was to watch Joe and Marie was to get dinner together until I got back. As I went out the door, he was seated beside his son and Marie was in the kitchen. An hour and a half later she met me at the door to tell me that Joe had experienced a gran mal seizure while I was gone and dad sat beside him blissfully unaware of what was going on. Gran mals can be noisy episodes and Marie heard the noise in the kitchen. She came charging into the front room just as Joe was coming out of it and hollered at her dad. The rest of the night, Wence over and over repeated that he had not been aware. Well excuse me! As noisy as that episode was how in the name of heaven could he not have been aware? These kinds of things happened so often that I finally learned that he was not to be trusted with child care of any kind. What a sad commentary on his parenting but I doubt that he was affected at all. As soon as she was old enough, he expected Marie to take over the parenting of her sibs if I was not available.

I bet the spouses of A/A individuals can all relate to this incident. The electronic filter for our oil furnace had a five year warranty on it. It is now seven years past warranty and we are still arguing about replacement. According to him it works fine. NOT!! The greasy residue on the walls and windows and the black colored grease that is on the cheesecloth that I put over the vents has nothing to do with the furnace filter. It is caused by the fact that I have on occasion lighted a scented candle to help ease the sulfur odor he leaves everywhere. That I have not lighted one of those candles in over three years isn't even in the picture. Now if this is true why is the cheesecloth over the bedrooms vents and other rooms in the house black too? Once something is in this man's head it is planted forever. Whether it makes normal sense is entirely beside the point. Sometimes I wonder why I try and then I remember that God put this man in my life for some reason that I can not fathom.

It is a declared need that he must have tomatoes from his garden available as long as possible. Once the temperature dips below fifty degrees at night, he wraps his plants in clear plastic and sticks the those scented candles he has declared off limits in the house, inside the plastic covers. I often wonder what goes through the neighbors minds when they see what he is doing

Don't forget that Wence is also a theological expert on our religious convictions. In his day, Catholic colleges expected the students to have minor in philosophy in order to graduate. That minor in his mind made him the most knowledgable soul of all those he knows regardless of the faith profession. I was reared being taught that any person can access Heaven if he truly believes that his religion is correct and he lives according to its precepts. Not true in Wence's world. Any one who was not Catholic was questionable and anyone who bad-mouthed a Catholic was anti Catholic. That the person in question might have some bad marks against him never counted. It went without saying that if a person was Catholic that automatically made him a good person. Some of the most morally questionable people I have ever met were self righteous Catholics who were nominal believers at best.

He has never understood that surnames in this country are not an indication of religious conviction. That premise may have held some validity in the early part of the last century but with the wide cultural diversity now in place that simply is no longer true. Try arguing that point with Wence and it is like bumping your head against brick walls.

There is a program in place in our church called, Disciples in Mission. Small groups of about ten or twelve people meet in private homes to discuss the Bible and study ways to apply it to the precepts of our faith. Wence regularly goes to this group and never comes away without having challenged someone in the group about some statement or other. He will come home and tell me that none of these folks are educated, none of them understand their religion and he has to keep them on the straight and narrow as regards church teaching. I have often wondered how he could possibly know that these folks are not educated. As for keeping them on the straight and narrow that would be as Wence defines it. Since he is not ordained and does not actively involve himself in any of the parish activities, I feel it is the height of supreme arrogance to assume that his faith knowledge is superior. What right does he have to be everyone's moral judge?

When I was growing up one of the ways my parents kept us children focused on the essence of Sunday services was to ask for an explanation of the homily when we returned home. I have many times asked Wence for as assessment of the homily and he has never been able to do that. I became aware early on that during the homily Wence was always mentally somewhere else. In fact some times he has come home and confessed to me that he was not aware of the entire service that day. I respond in a shocked tone that he was not fulfilling his Catholic duty if he was not aware of what was going on. That shocked tone was always enough to send him back for the next service. Was he aware the second time around? I have no idea and I always chose not to ask.

When I was available to go with him to Church I usually came home in a very frustrated mood. Common prayer is something that Wence can not participate in with any degree of accuracy.

During the petition sessions people ask for help from the Lord and the congregation responds, 'Lord hear our prayer.' Before the congregation has said the word Lord, Wence has finished the sentence. He is always way ahead of the congregation in any other group prayer too. I have heard him finish a prayer three sentences before the congregation does. Trying to stay with the congregation when he is beside me and does that is impossible. So when he joins in verbal prayer the easiest solution for me is to remain silent.

When the children were growing up and Wence was only available one calendar Sunday a month we would go to the liturgy that had been adapted to the needs of the 'challenged' population. I am sure that the children gained from this but it was my task to see that Joe was safe from the possibility of seizure related falls, and to see that Laura had enough opportunity to use the restroom. New environments have always given her a nervous bladder and it was wise to carry a clothing change for each of them. Wence would park himself in a pew and that was the last time he was aware of his kids until it was time to leave. He never noticed if Joe seizured or if Laura didn't quite make it to the restroom. Regularly he expounded on our obligation to take the children to this service. Why was this a mutual obligation when he was only a physical presence?

I told him that I didn't think God expected us to be doing this and nearly lost my head for having an opinion. For as polite as he is to women in general, I have never understood why he has such a hard time accepting that women can have valid opinions He just wouldn't listen and finally we talked to the pastor at the specialized liturgy and he said, "always welcome but never obligated." And Wence actually accepted that statement. It is such a relief that I no longer have to put over fifty miles on the car in an effort to fetch Joe to this liturgy. It is so much easier to just deal with Laura on these occasions. Even so, Wence still parks himself in a pew and on return home will ask me what the homily was about. If he is too proud to wear his hearing aids then I see no reason why I should need to do any explaining. Does that make me selfish? Maybe, but some days his attitudes are just too much to deal with. And I don't think God expects the impossible but only that I try.

Autism is a condition in which the majority of individuals have sensory problems now commonly called, 'sensory integration deficit Either the sensory system is so lacking in sensitivity that one is not aware that there is a sensory system or it is so overwhelming in that hearing and other sensory systems are as acute as an animal's might be. So either, the person smells nothing or is overcome because he can smell everything in his extended environment. This is why I do not wear perfumes around the family, why Wence does not use deodorant ever, and why he rarely washes his hands. In some sensory areas Wence is super sensitive and in others he lacks any awareness. Somehow over the years he has learned to compensate and therefore does not understand when his children are on sensory overload. This is especially true in the auditory area and he had no patience when sound would send Laura into a tantrum or Joe would stim in an out of control manner. I knew both behaviors were blocking mechanisms but I could not get him to accept that.

AS Marie matured and felt comfortable telling me about her perceptions of the world, I was so stunned that she had coped so well. She explained why she had begged for her own car. It seems that all those human smells on the bus were so overpowering that she was actually sick to her stomach and would get off the bus several blocks from home so that the fresh air could settle her stomach. Once she had her own vehicle she pointed out that she never wanted to deal with the 'great unwashed ever again' I guess a busload of people could smell like the great unwashed.

I had been in the basement, and came very quietly into the kitchen and was not making any sounds as I watched the birds through the window. The girls were in the living room watching television when Marie called for my attention. I asked how she knew I was in the kitchen. She said that she smelled me. Smelled me? I was surprised by her comment and she was dumbfounded to learn that I did not equate a smell with her. She then informed me that everyone has their own peculiar smell and that as a small child that was often how she identified people. She thought that was a normal process and that all people smelled things the way that she did.

Did Wence have this kind of sensitive system? I suspect he did and that since there was no help when he was a child he learned to cope by tuning out not only his sensory system but also his emotions. By tuning out and shutting down, he kept himself intact but that did not do much for his social skills.

His good friend who has known Wence since second grade has told us so much about Wence's childhood since I could never get Wence to tell me anything. There would be no reason for his friend to exaggerate so I do believe what he has told us. It seems that my spouse started school with a very serious accent; that made him the scapegoat for all the school's bullies. Having had no social training up to the beginnings of school time made him extremely shy and because he was so blonde and fair, if the teacher called on him the poor child turned all shades of red. Within a couple of years the teachers simply quit calling on him to recite. By the end of high school, he had lost his accent, but had discovered serious drinking in an effort to soothe his sensory system. He told me that his father used to say to him, 'if the cows can come home at night why can't you?'

Going home which was a seven mile walk was not a wise choice for one in a snockered condition. His friends, the few that he had, tended to keep him in town at one of their homes until the next morning. In spite of terrible hangovers the young man never missed a Sunday church service. I am not sure what that seems to indicate.

Auditory overload was definitely a part of Wence's growing up efforts. Otherwise how do you explain the way he has managed to tune out the world so much so that he isn't even aware when someone stands right beside him and speaks directly into his ear? None of the children could tune out sound that well and so auditory overload would precipitate some odd behaviors that were in reality a coping mechanism. That he should have been compassionate and understanding was not on his awareness screen, and sad to say we did have shouting matches over his desire to smack the kid that was on overload. Marie once threatened to call the cops if he ever touched any of them in that way and he backed off his immature behavior for that day. Later he again excused himself and I had to tell him that it was sometimes hard to believe that he was the adult. His inordinate pride in his college degree was always on the agenda and on more than one occasion I had to tell him to put that 'degree' to appropriate use. That would include allowing other people to have thoughts and opinions that differed from his. It is quite remarkable that the longer he is in retirement the more I.Q, points I lose. He now manages everyone else' s thoughts and moral convictions.

Any statement about things he has no knowledge of are a sure way to start a verbal battle. Because he is so sure that I am losing brain power, it is a given at least in his mind that I will not have the needed intellect to arrange his burial process. Very seldom do I challenge his crackpot observations because if I do I risk a violent reaction from him. That kind of tension just isn't worth it even though he should be challenged.

When he objected to a hug from me against his shoulders, he snapped that I should know he doesn't like being touched. My response was to ask him why then did he get married. In retrospect I now realize that touching was his forte. He could touch if he so desired but it was off limits to the rest of the family especially if they wanted to touch him in any way.

When I insisted that he and Marie go to the Czech Republic to visit newly discovered first cousins of his he said no way. Marie told him that she intended to have a relationship with those people even if he didn't and that she would go by herself. No female relative of his was going to be so daring so he agreed to go. They got on the plane and flew to Chicago and stayed the night to make the non-stop connection the next day. Marie later told me that he spent that entire night moaning and groaning and griping and asking himself why he ever got married. Since he had made similar comments in the past, I was not particularly surprised. It fit his attitude. On more than one occasion when he was two sheets to the wind from booze he regularly told Marie that she should never consider marriage because it wasn't worth it. There was one too many comments like that and I began to withdraw all the efforts I was putting into making him happy. I realized that it would never be possible. My full time focus became the children. Did he notice? Probably not! Did he care? I don't think so. Eventually it came down to being two adults who lived in the same house.

I was always stunned by his assumptions that his children would lead their adult lives as he ordered. When I pointed out that they might have their own agenda for adulthood, his response was that he was the father and they would do as he wished. Did his father tell him what to do as an adult? Well, golly, gee that was entirely different. Why would that have been so different? Do you see the autistic reasoning here? Logic simply has no part in how he views his world

In the 90's a concept surfaced in Australia that gave non-verbal challenged people an opportunity to communicate. The process, known as facilitated communication made a major impact on my children. Laura was invited to be in a presentation in which this concept was presented. She caught on quickly and we came home to a new life. Using a small 5x7 cardboard sheet with the alphabet printed on it, she began to type her thoughts. After a few days of finding out that my daughter was a whole lot smarter than anyone was giving her credit for, Marie suggested we try the same approach on Joe. Amazingly this process worked on Josef too. He told us that he had learned to read from watching Sesame Street. Laura indicated that she could not remember when she could not read. The poster that reads 'No voice does not equal no brains.' is now one that I sincerely believe should hang on the classroom walls of all schools and on the walls in the homes of anyone who parents a challenged child.

Once communication became a two way process we were amazed at what Joe and Laura knew about the world. When confronted about the knowledge they seemed to have accrued over the years, Joe was quick to comment, "I listen, I learn." And Laura was able to say, 'Me too."

There was a real trick in learning to hold the hand firmly, without taking control of the communication that they were sending out. Since Wence could not seem to grasp the correct way to do this he would not believe that his children were saying anything. It has taken over fifteen years for him to believe that facilitated communication can be a valid concept. He now believes his children especially if they happen to say something that is in compliance with what he believes. He is especially livid if they speak of how people have mistreated them over the years.

This area had a strong earthquake now known as the spring break quake and a couple days later we had to go to the basement to complete a task and were surprised to see water all along the perimeter of one wall. Wence's comment that Laura must has 'pissed' her pants was so bizarre that I had to say, "Don't be stupid." There must have been fifty plus gallons of water along that wall. It turned out that the quake had cracked the water heater severely enough that all the water had drained into a nearby floor sump Thank goodness there were willing neighbors to help him replace that tank. When I told other folks about his comment that Laura was the culprit for all that water, they were able to joke about how she must have had a magnificent bladder and we never knew. Those kinds of jokes were always appreciated because it helped to take the bite out of his off the wall comments.

Lost and misplaced tools were always Joe's fault. Now since Joe was never allowed to be mobile unless Marie or I was beside him and since he never was in the basement or near the tool table, the rest of us could never understand why he thought that Joe had taken his tools.

This man has a phobia about doctors and refused for many years to go to one. Finally when I told him that he owed it to his family to stay healthy until they were grown. That was enough to get him to agree to a yearly checkup. That no doctor would do this for free griped him no end and after a colonoscopy he refused to ever go back. He thought that the female doctor was a poor excuse of humanity and when I chastised him for that and asked why it was ok for women to always go to a man doctor. He told me that was something entirely different and besides that was the way it was supposed to be. Was he ever able to explain that reasoning? Not in the least.

Factory work was a hard physical job and after several years, Wence developed a very pronounced limp. I am just fine he told me. I assumed that he knew how he felt and sort of ignored the obvious until one day he told me that one entire leg was going numb. I wasted no time in getting him to a doctor and surgery was needed on his lower back. For the three days that he was in the hospital, he obsessed over the fact that he was not having a bowel movement. Repeated explanation by the staff just didn't register. He couldn't understand that the pain medication and anesthesia were the reason for no B. M. He was off work for eight weeks and went back after a neurological evaluation as thirty percent permanent partial paralysis. In short order he back on full duty and three years later the same problem recurred. Since he was self medicating with alcohol to relieve the pain he was telling me he did not have, this time around I got him to the doctor a lot quicker. A second surgery was necessary and this time he was off for three months before he was released to go back to light duty. A check up six weeks back on the job revealed that there was not enough healing and it was determined that he needed to retire. To leave that factory after thirty plus years was so traumatic to him that the idea of spending some quality spousal togetherness just didn't compute.

And I have too much pride to become a beggar. Shortly before he retired he started to wear a leg brace and is such a rough neck with it that in a few short years he had to have it replaced. It has become an absolute necessity for him to wear the brace in order to be able to walk and to keep himself balanced. He has never admitted to any mental shortcomings and he sure isn't going to admit that he is anything physically less than perfect. I let him keep his illusions and to make sure I keep my sanity I refuse to play constant care taker of either him or his home. Not only does he need the leg brace for balance, whenever he is moving he always hangs onto the wall. After the surgeries, hanging onto the wall was such a constant that I finally had to ask why. So I don't fall was his response and for as sure footed as he has always been that was a surprise. Did he really need to hang onto the wall or was it faulty perception? I think it is definitely visual problems. He has never been able to let go of this problem so there is a greasy messy section along every wall in the house where he puts his hands. Oh I wipe it down from time to time but overall it is next to impossible to get rid of his particular handprints. I want some sort of life so I will not follow him around 24/7 as his personal janitor. We have all learned to adjust to a less than spotless house. I have learned to accept his dogma that in the moral scheme of things God does not demand clinical cleanliness. He is happy that way and when he is content the rest of us do not have to walk on eggshells

Over the years I have read and read and reread every piece of information that I could get my hands on in regards to autism. Much to my chagrin when the kids were small there wasn't much out there about the condition and certainly none on adults with this condition or with other disabilities also present. Even today there is not much on the elder adults who deal with this syndrome. I have more or less been flying by the seat of my pants when dealing with Wence's many difficulties all these years.

Back to the concept of cleanliness…that a certain level of clean was a practicality in no way dented Wence's awareness level. Let me explain with a couple examples. One spring day , after spending time in the muddy garden, he came tromping in to use the bathroom, without bothering to wipe the mud from the bottom or sides of his shoes. I had just finished shampooing the rug with a rented machine so the carpet was still damp. Well, why would that matter? The man left mud tracks all the way across the carpet and down the hall. When he came out and saw me standing there with tears running down my face, he asked what was wrong. I pointed to his tracks and he snapped, "I told you not to put in carpet." and went on his way. It took me several hours to clean all that mud and he could not understand why I was very cool toward him for several days.

Bringing produce in from the garden is another habit that drives me to the brink of insanity. I appreciate the fresh produce but after he hoses it off outside, he brings it immediately inside which means that water is dripping everywhere. When I have objected he always says that it will dry. Well doesn't it occur to him that a puddle of water might be dangerous; that it could cause someone to slip and be injured? He has forever thought that I am too too picky. Why should he dry his hands on a towel after washing them? It is easier just to shake that excess water onto the floor. Is it because that is how things were done in that home where the floor covering was actually the sub flooring planks?

In the beginnings of our marriage, he complained that over clean was unhealthy. After he attends to personal hygiene each morning, I have to follow his pathway into the bathroom. A fully grown seal would probably not leave as many water tracks as he does. I need to use a highly absorbent towel to soak up all the water he leaves on the counter, a glass cleaner for the mirror and a cleaner for the back splash which is always splattered with the mess his mouth leaves from tooth brushing. Then there is always the sink that needs a major clean up after he is done.

In our inner circle, there is a very active grapevine that manages to advise me of some of Wence's declarations. One that has consistently surprised me; is that he considers himself an inadequate father. Maybe down in his subconscious he knows that he not only should have done better but that he could have if he had put out the effort. Of course, it would be extremely difficult to try to do things that you had never been taught. And, he had no male role model when it came to learning parenting skills

Because of no role model and his autistic expectations, especially concerning his son, I knew that once he retired there would be no way that Wence and his son could co-exist peacefully under the same roof. What a terrible burden for me to solve. About five years before the expected retirement date, I began to explore the possibilities of moving Josef into a group home. So many of the so called 'quality' homes were not and in my opinion had no clue as to how to deal with the autistic population. The closer it got to retirement the more I could see that Josef and his dad could not live in the same environment. His father's expectations for Joe were so unrealistic that I finally put in a desperate call to the person who was the county office that dealt with the developmentally delayed population. They in turn referred me to an office in Salem that sent an examiner to our house. The fellow was very supportive of what I told him and while Wence tried to contribute, the man kept sending strange looks at Wence and then would look back at me.

The state considered us to be in crisis and that is the only reason we were able to find a group home facility for Joe. We were referred to an organization that had an excellent reputation in the county and after careful examination decided that this would be appropriate for Joe. It was hard to give up the care of my child to someone else but we tried to smooth the way by telling Joe that this was a move that would prove he was not only an adult but a man.

When he moved into Sundial, I cried for a week. We checked on him every day for a month until I was satisfied that he was adjusting. Then the girls and I began taking him for an outing every other week. After a couple months at the home I asked him if the staff was taking good care of him. When he replied that they did better than family I knew things would be OK and that he had probably adjusted as much as would be possible with a 30% staff turnover. Because staff was so young and some so hyper there were accidents that I thought could have been avoided. There were many times in the past seven years that I have wanted to screech at someone for some of the things I have seen but Wence and I have both learned to bite the tongue when speaking out really will not improve things. Probably the biggest gripe we have is the staff constantly on their personal cell phones but I understand that this is now a common situation in the work place. As you might have guessed this family has a big problem with the proliferation of cell phones as we remember life when even a regular phone was not commonplace.

Wence goes to the group home every Sunday to visit Joe and I think it is some kind of belated attempt on his part to make up for all that he did not do when his son lived at home. I have asked Joe about his dad visiting every Sunday and he said that dad does not come to see him. Rather he spends all the time talking to staff.

How does Joe feel about this? He states that dad's conversations are so embarrassing that most of the time he has to go to his room. Will I ever tell Wence what his son has said? No. Nothing could be gained from telling him.

We have asked Joe if he would ever want to return to living with his family and he has said, "Not as long as dad is alive." That breaks my heart but I understand where he is coming from.

I certainly came from a broken family. I understand that the first generation children of immigrants, especially those who came from eastern Europe as mine did were poorly educated and poorly parented. Those parents did the best they could with the knowledge they had at that time. They gave the best effort that they knew. I have repeated this over and over to so many people I know who came from immigrant backgrounds. And still today after another generation is almost past there is still great bitterness. How very sad that so many people are stuck in their pasts. I suspect God wants us to be moving forward. That explains so much about Wence that I wish I would have known in the beginnings of our marriage. It would have made him easier to understand and maybe I might have had the wisdom to handle him and our marriage very differently.

Just recently Wence admitted to me that he came from a very dysfunctional family and then expounded on his parents. He can't prove it but strongly suspects that his parents had an arranged marriage. It was not uncommon to have great age differences between spouses in the early part of the twentieth century, but for heaven sake why would parents arrange a marriage to a man nearly as old as they were for their daughter? Three children in three years put a severe load on the wife as the last birth was the result of three days of severe labor that left a permanent disability on the mother in addition to the family proclamation that she was retarded. I never knew the woman but find it hard to believe that someone who could read and write in two languages, knew how to can food and sew would be retarded. Maybe it was a case of this assumption becoming a self- fulfilling prophecy. That seven mile distance from town made if especially difficult to keep in touch with family who lived in other nearby towns. Loneliness had to be a given

Wence remembers his father as a chronic negative grouch. He was actually an old man by the time Wence was old enough to have memories of him as he was fifty two when Wence came along. Do you realize how old that would have been in 1934? The man never felt well, (I suspect undiagnosed diabetes) When ever, he was asked how he felt he always replied in his native tongue…not good.

The man came to this country at the age of thirty, but his heart and soul remained forever attached to his native village. While he understood English fairly well, I have been told, that he preferred not to use it.

Wence remembers that his dad could not get the hang of driving a car. The guy had been an outstanding groomsman in the Old Country but coordinating a clutch and gas pedal on a car was beyond him. Transmissions were regularly torn out and in need of replacement

When he did manage to get the car in motion more often than not he could not control it and nosed into the ditch on many outings. Thank goodness, there were willing neighbors with tractors who came to pull that battered vehicle out of the ditch. Brother took over driving chores as soon as he was old enough

This father never let the lady of the house forget an accident that happened when Wence was a toddler. He got in the way when she was chopping wood for the kitchen stove and he lost the first two fingers on his left hand. He does not remember the episode but his dad forever after always remarked to her, "You made a cripple of your son." Can you imagine what that did to the poor woman's self-esteem? It certainly would not have done much for Wence either to always be hearing that kind of garbage. Wence grew up never knowing anything different and was capable enough to be able to enlist and serve in the military.

When the couple had married, her father and brothers constructed a small cottage type shelter with the assumption that the man would put the finishing touches on the place. According to Wence that never happened and what was there never received a bit of maintenance over

the years. How that man expected his wife to cook and clean and rear children without running water, indoor plumbing or electricity is almost beyond belief. That lady, in my books, deserves unending accolades. There was never any paternal parenting and according to Wence, this man knew nothing about anything. He says that he received more parenting from his older brother (older by three years) than he ever got from his father. How weird! This father was never available in any sense of the word. It was always mother and the children while he was off doing his own thing. Does this sound like an autism/Asperger man? Did he pass some of these anomalies onto his offspring? I now strongly suspect so.

Given this background, it is remarkable how well Wence has done for himself. Not only does he maintain his home when needed, he has learned to do the repairs to our vehicles, and tries very hard to be a good neighbor especially to those in need. Because he was especially close to his mother and knows how badly she was treated, he has developed a tender caring for the elder ladies in our church who have no one. He has gone and done yard work for them, he gives them excess garden produce and while he sometimes misreads the ladies I have always encouraged him in this endeavor.

Some parts of this narrative may sound like Wence has insurmountable problems, and in many ways his social ineptness will always be part and parcel of who he is. Has this life been difficult? Without a doubt but I have to remember that there is a whole world out there where people have more difficulties than this family.

If sometimes I seem to be overwhelmed, I am also grateful to have this man in my life. Because of his many social disabilities, he has kept me grounded in reality. How so?

Guiding him through the maze of the English language has always been a constant. Constantly urging him to not expect his daughters to behave like sons is a never- ending chore. Making him understand that his adult children have a right to question his assumptions and a right to make their own mistakes is a daily ongoing task. Getting him to make choices that require an immediate decision has never been on the menu. He can not make any kind of decision without dissecting it over and over and over. By the time he makes a choice the reason for the choice would no longer be available. Example….Shortly after Joe was in the group home it was discovered that his tonsils were so large as to be interfering with his breathing. Recommendation was removal and Wence was absolutely convinced that this would cause the demise of our son because when he was in grade school over fifty years ago a classmate had bled to death after this kind of surgery. That it was fifty years later and technology so vastly improved did not even enter his mind. If it happened once then it was surely going to happen again. In the end, I had to make the decision for removal without his input. Joe recovered just fine.

Theory of mind is a condition peculiar to those on the autistic spectrum. This condition surfaces in Wence is odd little snippets. Probably the one that makes me the most nuts is his attitude that I must think about the world in exactly the same way that he does. In spite of our similar moral and ethical values, I certainly do not have the same thoughts as he does nor do I assume that his thoughts are mine. I do not know what he is thinking and I would never expect him to know what I am thinking. Theory of mind also seems to assume that the rest of the world will function the way he not only expects it to but demands that it will. If something does not happen that way he prefers then it is just plain wrong and he has every right to bad mouth whatever it was. Just recently he stated that he had a feeling that the young man visiting the neighbor across the street was a leech and that this particular neighbor could not afford heat. How could he possibly know that? Of course he didn't   Let's not forget the most recent social anomaly. JESUS LOVES ME is a favorite song among the developmentally delayed population and it is sung often at the disabilities liturgy. Somewhere this man got it in his head that country singer Tennessee Ernie Ford was the composer. I was adamant that this song DID NOT originate with Tennessee Ernie and Wence got downright angry with me. There are days when the constant negative bad mouthing of everything just gets to me too much and I find solace in reading the Scriptures . If he sees me with the Bible, he tends to leave me alone. There are many times when silence truly is golden.

When the children were in school I often felt that I was banging my head against a brick wall and was relieved when that part of our lives was over. After thirty five years , I am still banging my head against that brick wall when it comes to bringing Wence into the world of reality and awareness. I have never made him happy nor have his children simply because we refuse to go into his world. He is so content there that he refuses to be anywhere else. His world pleases him but he should not expect the rest of us to choose to be in that world unless we want to. That world is so confining that I can not imagine the rest of us living with him in that little hole

Not too long ago a male friend who grew up in a large city and in a different culture told me that his father never taught him anything about how to be a man. That set up a resonating thought in my head that had me finally making sense of my spouse's anomalies

It is certainly a given that you can not learn what you were not taught. That seems to me to be the essence of being a parent. You nurture your child so that he can make his way in the world and perhaps be in a better place than you were.

However, what if neither parent understood how to do that? Where does that leave the child? Struggling in a vacuum that makes no sense to him and further alienates his already confused sensory system. What parent allows a small child to wander all day without ever checking to see if all was well.

Sloshing around the barnyard as if it were a perfect playground is a concept that makes today's parent cringe. Giving a small child free range to wander the entire neighborhood, and allowing that child to swim unattended in a river, was not the credible thing to do. Letting that child wander through an entire winter in wet shoes because boots were too expensive to be on the budget was certainly not good health sense as it had to be a contributing factor to the chronic tonsillitis that occurred every winter. Was it also a contributing factor in the adult hearing loss?

Wence's constant harping that the family farm was the ideal place makes sense if that is where he was least overwhelmed by sensory overload.

So then, this has been a story that sounds perhaps like a fairy tale but I assure you, it has been accurate. When I first entered the world of autism I had absolutely no idea what I was in for. I knew that the man I married was uniquely different. How different was going to be the force that drove our marriage and our life. Was it difficult? Probably the most difficult part of my life. Had I known how it would be I would probably have run as far away as fast as I could. Once I made that commitment I knew I would stay…for better or worse. So we have had lots of bad things go on but there has always been that smart individual who made life a challenge just because his intellect was so different.

There are researchers who in the last few years are declaring that autism can be cured. This is a statement I take with a grain of salt. Perhaps if there is early diagnosis and immediate intervention a cure is a possibility. The few possibly recovered adults that I have met over time are indeed able to fit into the world of 'normal' but they retain an intensity that still labels them as different. Different is acceptable today where it was once sneered at by all segments of society.

What about those autistic adults today who range from 40 to 70+ in age and have never had any sort of intervention? Is it possible that some researcher out there is finding a way to reach this population? Would this group of folks even want an intervention when they have managed thus far own their own?

Autism has defined my life, my marriage and my family for thirty five years. It has colored every aspect of every thing I have done. At times it has been heart breaking and at times I did not think I could continue. A strong faith has been the base on which our life is built and it is that which has taken us through the tough times. I can't imagine that life could have been any easier and I can't possibly imagine how my life might have been without this family.

Focusing on them has taught me that love is always unconditional and unending and that I am blessed for having them in my life.